for

Alexandra

Annie Kay

Ardith

Bonnie

Buddy

Catherine

Cayetana

Charlo

David

Deej

Diana

Diane

Erika

Ewan

Fiona

Gary

Gillian

Gordon

Hubie

Jackson

Jaime

Jasper

Jay

Julie

Kenneth

Kier

Lesley

Lindy

Lisa Toba

Liza

Macy

Marc

Marsha

Martha

Michael

Paula

Penn

Phyllis Tani

Piojo

Rebecca

Richard

Roseann

Sabrina

Samlet

Sara Ann

Spencer

Susan

Sylvia

Tom

Tomas

Trippie

always giving,
Aunt Lillian

Phaidon Press Limited
Regent's Wharf
All Saints Street
London N1 9PA

Phaidon Press Inc.
180 Varick Street
New York, NY 10014

www.phaidon.com

This edition © 2008 Phaidon Press Limited
First published in 1961 by Harper & Brothers Publishers

ISBN 978 0 7148 4873 0 (UK/US edition)

A CIP catalogue record for this book is
available from the British Library.

Designed by Bob Gill
Jacket photograph by Susan Greenburg
Printed in China

a Balloon
for a Blunderbuss

Bob Gill/Alastair Reid

Φ

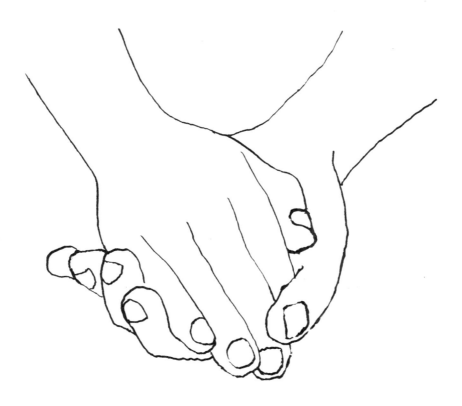

"I have a butterfly in my hands.

What will you give me for my butterfly?"

"I will give you

a wishbone."

"What would I do
with a wishbone?"
"Well, you could trade
it for a kite with a
tail . . . or a Chinese
lantern. Or, if you
like, for

a flag.

Then you could trade your flag
for a straw hat, and for a straw
hat, you could get

a green umbrella

or a sea horse."

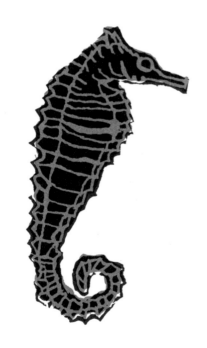

"I could trade my sea horse for

a row of tin soldiers

or ninety-seven stamps

or six hundred and fifty toothpicks

or a shirt with my name on it.

But I think I'd wait and trade it for

a ship in a bottle.

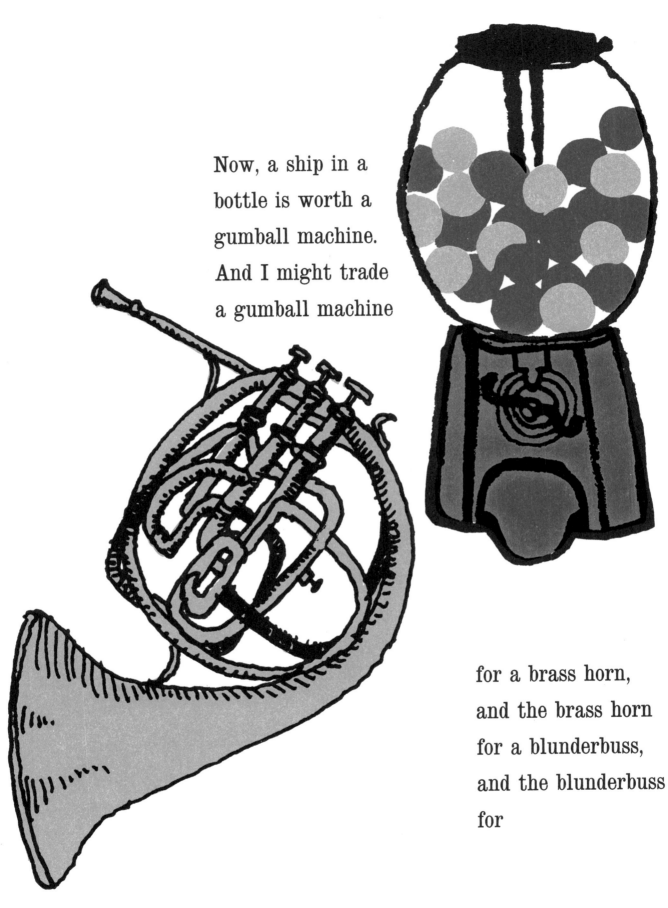

Now, a ship in a
bottle is worth a
gumball machine.
And I might trade
a gumball machine

for a brass horn,
and the brass horn
for a blunderbuss,
and the blunderbuss
for

a balloon I could fly in.
Then, when I was tired of flying, I could trade it

for a trolley car of my own,

and the trolley car
for two rocking horses
and a small zoo with

a lion. Then, I could trade my zoo for

a tall tower.
(I might keep
one rocking
horse.) Then,
in time, I
could trade
my tall tower
          for

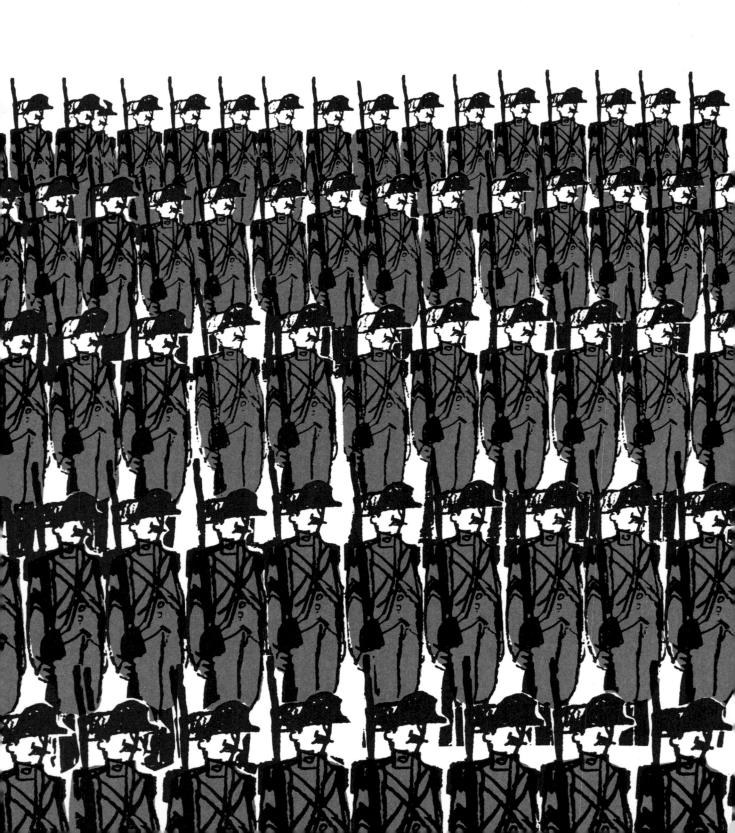

a small army. (Imagine, I'd own an army.)
And the army for a little town.

And the town for a rushing waterfall or
a whole forest with thousands of trees.

What would I trade my forest for?

Perhaps eight mountains with snow on top

or eleven towering icebergs

or an overgrown jungle

or a desert that never ended

or two stars.

But I think I would
rather have

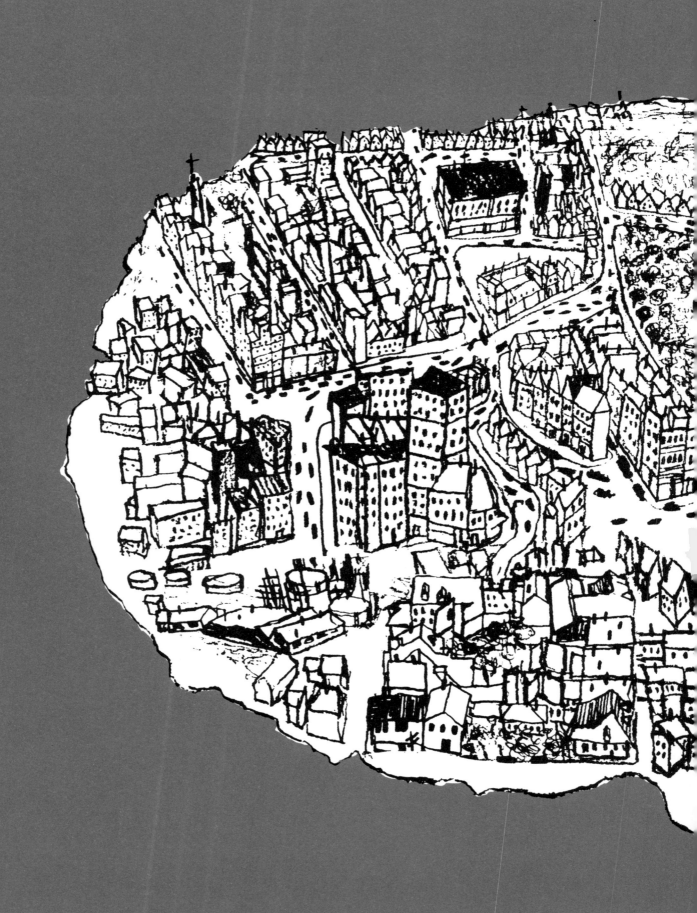

I would trade and trade and trade, and in the end I would own

EVERYTHING!

Think of it!

I began with
a butterfly
in my hands and
now I own
EVERYTHING!"

"Show me your butterfly."

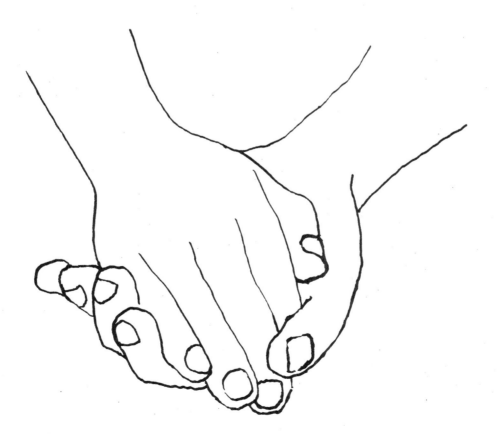

"Look!"

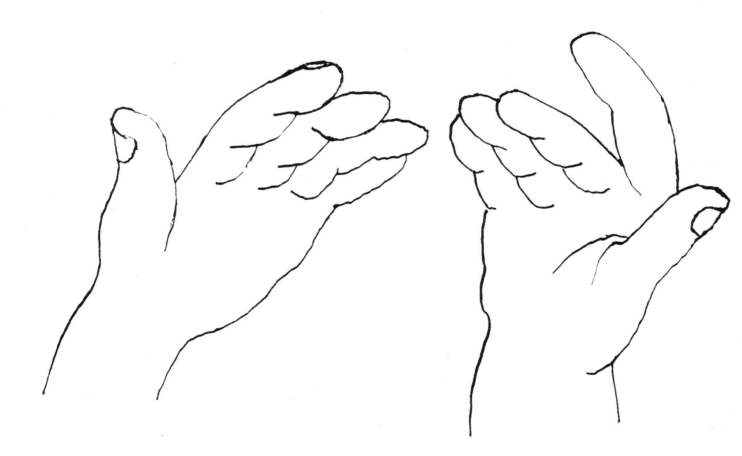

If you've enjoyed reading this book,
why not read What Colour Is Your World?,
also by Bob Gill.

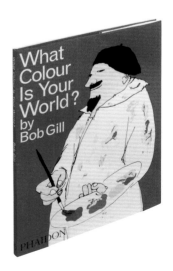

ISBN: 978 0 7148 4850 1